BETH
the Tracker

Adam and Alex Mittendorf

Illustrations by
Maren Hampton

AuthorHouse™
1663 Liberty Drive
Bloomington, IN 47403
www.authorhouse.com
Phone: 1-800-839-8640

Published by AuthorHouse 09/26/2012

ISBN: 978-1-4772-7021-9 (sc)

Library of Congress Control Number: 2012917123

Any people depicted in stock imagery provided by Thinkstock are models,
and such images are being used for illustrative purposes only.
Certain stock imagery © Thinkstock.

Illustrations by Maren Hampton

authorHOUSE®

Beth the Tracker

Adam and Alex Mittendorf

Illustrations by
Maren Hampton

Chapter 1 - The Beginning

Our story is about a Springer Spaniel named Beth. Beth lives with a happy, loving family. There is a mom, a dad and two boys named Adam and Alex. The boys are in fourth and second grades and love playing with their dog.

One Saturday morning at breakfast, the family was talking about how they could not find 2 library books. Adam said that he looked all around the bedrooms and even under his bed. Alex said that he looked in the play room and in the closets. Mom looked around the kitchen and Dad looked in the garage and in the cars. No one was able to find the books anywhere.

Adam and Alex knew the books had to be in the house, but they didn't know where. Oh where could those books be?

Beth was lying on her bed in the kitchen listening to her family talk about the missing library books. She knew that she could help, but she didn't know how.

When her family went to the grocery store, Beth leapt off her bed and walked around thinking about how she could help. She kept thinking and thinking as she walked around the house. Suddenly, she smells something different in the house. It is not a normal scent and she isn't sure what the smell belongs to. Beth follows her nose and sniffs around until she finds where the scent is coming from.

Beth has a great nose and works until she tracks down the scent. Wow! The scent is coming from THE BOOKS! How did those books get under the couch? I guess no one looked under there. She puts the books in her mouth and then puts them on the kitchen counter for her family to find.

When the family comes home, they find the books.

Chapter 2 - The SDA

Beth was very happy that she helped her family. But what Beth didn't know was that someone was watching her. Beth had never heard of the Secret Dog Agency or SDA and she didn't know how they helped people and dogs.

The SDA was looking for new agents. They liked how Beth was able to find the books for her family, so the top dog went to visit Beth when she was outside.

Stone looked around to make sure no one could hear or see him before talking to Beth.

When it was clear, Stone called out to Beth. Ruff! Ruff!

Beth was surprised; no other dogs had been in her backyard.

Stone told her that he was from the SDA and they wanted her to join the agency. Stone explained that the SDA was there to help people and other dogs.

Beth was excited and wanted to get started right away on the adventure.

Beth didn't know how to get to the SDA. Stone told her that she needed to use a secret tunnel to get there and the closest tunnel was just across the street.

Beth didn't know any secret agents, so who could it be? Stone told Beth that Bailey was an agent. Beth was very surprised that Bailey was in the SDA. They lived across the street from each other and talked between their yards every day. Bailey is really good at keeping a secret.

Stone and Beth used Bailey's secret tunnel to get to the SDA Headquarters or HQ. It was a fast trip. The HQ team told Beth that they would build her a secret tunnel while she was in training.

Stone and Beth took a tour of the building. The kitchen is on the first floor. Anyone can come in to get something to eat or drink at any time of the day or night. The SDA always has agents working, so HQ is always open. If you need to take something with you, there are doggie bags and water bottles to use.

Stone and Beth take the tube up to the second floor to walk around the gym. All training takes place in the gym. There are obstacles, climbing nets, swimming and a running track. Central Communications and Research is on the third floor.

In Central Communications, agents are watching monitors that show what the agents on assignment are doing around the world. Each agent has a secret camera on their collar, so that they can get in contact with Central Communications at anytime. Also, if an agent has any trouble, they contact Central Communications and they can find another agent to help them. Central Communications watches other secret cameras that are near where the agents live to look for people or dogs that have a problem that an agent could fix. In Research, the SDA is always creating new tools for the agents and researching ways to solve problems. Ronan is the agent in charge of Research.

Chapter 3 - Getting Started

Beth was a good dog at the SDA and she liked it a lot. Beth is a secret agent now and ready to help a lot of dogs and people.

One day, Beth is outside taking a nap. Her collar started beeping and Beth went inside her dog house to see what her assignment is. Beth presses the paw print on the wall to bring up a secret screen. The screen pops up, but it isn't working yet. There is a note that says it will start working in two days. Beth starts talking out loud and asks what she needs to do. Beth forgot that she needs to press the red button next to the paw print to open up her tunnel to the SDA HQ.

Beth goes into the tunnel and is at HQ in a couple of minutes. When she gets there, she goes to Central Communication to find out what she needs to do and who needs help.

Stone tells Beth that there is a dog in her neighborhood named Evie who is stuck inside and needs to go outside to the bathroom. Before leaving HQ, Beth visits Research to get a new gadget. Beth tells Ronan what she needs to do and Ronan has the perfect gadget for Beth. It is a lasso that Beth can use to open a sliding glass door. Beth thanks Ronan and heads back to the tunnel to take her back to her yard.

Once Beth gets back to her yard, she goes to Evie's house. Beth had never been there before, but her collar told her how to get there. When Evie sees Beth, she is so happy and tells her to hurry. Beth gets the lasso out and opens the door quickly. Evie runs out into the yard and goes to the bathroom. Then she thanks Beth for her help.

Beth is very excited that she was able to help and goes home with a smile on her face.

Chapter 4 - Problem Solved

The very next day, Beth was in her backyard again taking a nap. She always likes to take a nap laying in the grass with the sun on her. Beth hears another dog yelling for help. Beth gets up and leaves her yard to find the dog. When Beth finds Romey, she is very upset and crying. Beth asks her what is wrong and Romey tells her that she is lost and scared.

Beth tells Romey that she is part of the SDA and will help her get home. They go to Beth's yard and Beth calls Central Communications. Beth tells Central Communications what has happened and asks how she can help Romey get home.

Central Communications tells Beth that she needs to visit Ronan in Research for help. Beth tells Romey that she is safe in her yard and that she will be right back. Beth takes her secret tunnel to HQ and goes immediately to Research. Ronan is busy at work on new gadgets. Beth tells Ronan the story and asks if he has any ideas on how to help Romey get back home to her family. Ronan thinks about all the gadgets that he has created and thinks about how he could put some together to create a new gadget to help Romey. Ronan tells Beth that he will be back in an hour. He goes into the lab to get started. Beth visits the kitchen and gets a doggie bag for lunch for her and Romey.

Beth takes her secret tunnel back to her yard where Romey is waiting for her. Romey is still scared, but Beth tells her that Ronan is going to help and that she will be home before dinner. Romey and Beth share the lunch that Beth brought back from HQ.

After they are done, Romey takes a nap while Beth goes back to HQ. Ronan is waiting for Beth and said that he has a gadget that will help. Ronan brings out a hat that has a funny top. Ronan tells Beth that Romey needs to put on the hat and the hat will know where she lives from her memories. A map will show up on top of the hat for you to follow to take her home. Great idea!

Beth goes back to her yard and finds Romey sleeping in the sun. She is excited to see Beth return and thinks the hat she is carrying looks silly. Beth tells Romey how it works and Romey puts it on.

The hat starts working and after a few minutes a map shows up over Romey's head. Beth and Romey leave the yard and start following the map. It is a long walk, but Romey starts to recognize the houses and they find her home. And just as Beth said it isn't even time for dinner yet.

Romey is so excited. She thanks Beth and goes to her yard.

Beth puts the hat on and it gives her a map to find her way back to her home. Another great day for Beth!

Made in the USA
Lexington, KY
27 August 2013